D0453033

V.C.E. School
row
rston
8QF
05 31365

THE BIG HILL

PLAYGROUND

Hogs Back Books
The Stables
Down Place
Hogs Back
Guildford GU3 1DE
www.hogsbackbooks.com
Text copyright © 2010 Karen Hodgson
Illustrations copyright © Sally Anne Lambert
The moral right of Karen Hodgson to be identified as the author and
Sally Anne Lambert to be identified as the illustrator of this work has been asserted.
First published in Great Britain in 2010 by Hogs Back Books Ltd.

All rights reserved. No reproduction, copy or transmission
of this publication may be made without written permission.
No part of this publication may be reproduced, stored in a retrieval system,
or transmitted in any form or by any means, electronic, mechanical, photocopying,
recording or otherwise without the prior permission of the publisher.

Printed in China
ISBN: 978-1-907432-02-6
British Library Cataloguing-in-Publication Data.
A catalogue record for this book is available from the British Library.
1 3 5 4 2

The Teeny-Weeny Walking Stick

Karen Hodgson ● Sally Anne Lambert

Hogs Back Books

For Harriet and Edward - KJH

For my daughter Katie - SAL

Hattie was doing her homework when Edward burst into the bedroom. "Quick Hattie, come and see!" he said, tugging at her jumper. "I've discovered something important!"

"What is it *this* time?" groaned Hattie as she tapped out numbers on her calculator. She was in the middle of a difficult sum and in no mood for one of Edward's 'discoveries'.

Edward waited for the tapping to stop before delivering his news. "I think there may be *little people* living at the bottom of the garden," he whispered.

"Don't be ridiculous Edward!" said Hattie. "Everyone knows there's no such thing as little people. Go away and play!"

But Edward didn't move. There *were* little people living at the bottom of his garden and he *knew* it. He gave Hattie one of his stubborn looks.

"Have you seen them?" asked Hattie irritably. She wanted to put an end to this nonsense.

Edward's face fell. He hadn't actually *seen* the little people, but he'd seen their *things*. "Pleeeease Hattie, come and look!"

Hattie sighed. "Ok, but first you'll have to bring me proof."

"No problem," said Edward and off he marched to the bottom of the garden.

Two sums later, Edward returned clutching something tightly.

"What's that?" asked Hattie, pointing to the silvery-white object poking out of Edward's chubby fingers.

"It's my proof," said Edward proudly. "It's a teeny-weeny walking stick. It belongs to the little people."

Hattie peered closely at Edward's newly found treasure. "That's not a walking stick," she scoffed. "It's just some old twig. It's fallen from the silver birch tree. You'll have to find better proof than that!"

Edward frowned. He placed the walking stick on his 'special shelf' and disappeared again to the bottom of the garden.

Three sums later Edward was back. "Look Hattie! I've found a teeny-weeny hat. It must belong to the little people," he said and opened his hand to reveal a perfectly formed miniature cap.

Hattie was not impressed. "That's not a hat. It's an acorn cup! It's fallen from the oak tree and the acorn has dropped out. You'll have to find better proof than that!"

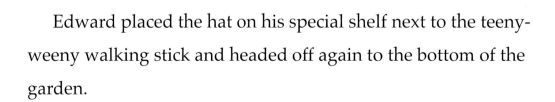

Edward placed the hat on his special shelf next to the teeny-weeny walking stick and headed off again to the bottom of the garden.

This time Hattie managed four sums before Edward appeared, gently stroking another treasure. "I've found some *real* proof this time Hattie," he said. "Look, it's a teeny-weeny pair of fluffy slippers! These *must* belong to one of the little people."

"Sorry Edward," said Hattie, shaking her head. "You haven't found a pair of fluffy slippers at all. Those are catkins. They've fallen from the pussy willow tree. You're wasting your time. You're not going to find any proof because

THERE

ARE

NO

LITTLE

PEOPLE!"

Edward couldn't believe it. He'd been sure that the fluffy slippers would convince Hattie. He placed them gently on his special shelf next to the teeny-weeny hat and the teeny-weeny walking stick, and again made his way to the bottom of the garden.

While he was gone, Hattie looked at all the treasures lined up on Edward's special shelf and laughed.

"Fancy believing in little people," she thought to herself and returned to her homework.

Hattie was just finishing her last sum when Edward strode confidently into the room.

"I've found it!" he exclaimed. "This time I've found *absolute* proof," and thrust his hand under Hattie's nose. "It's a teeny-weeny fairy wing. This must belong to the little people!"

Hattie was tired of this game. "Edward you are being silly. That is *not* a fairy wing. It's the seed from a sycamore tree. Don't you remember spinning them round like helicopters with Grandpa!"

Edward felt sad. He did remember playing helicopters with Grandpa. Perhaps Hattie was right after all – there were no unicorns, there were no ghosts, there were no flying saucers and there were no little people.

"I've finished my homework now," Hattie said when she saw Edward's glum face. "Would you like a game of football before bedtime?"

Edward beamed. He placed the fairy wing on his special shelf next to the teeny-weeny fluffy slippers, the teeny-weeny hat and the teeny-weeny walking stick. He picked up his ball and went back to the garden, where he beat Hattie five goals to three.

At eight o'clock Hattie and Edward were in bed. The moon shone down on the sleeping children and a gentle breeze blew through the open window.

Somewhere in her dreams, Hattie heard
a teeny-weeny voice coming from Edward's
special shelf. "I told you there were *big people*
living at the top of the garden!" it said.

The next morning when Hattie woke up, Edward was jumping up and down with excitement. He pulled her across to his special shelf. The teeny-weeny walking stick, the teeny-weeny hat, the teeny-weeny fluffy slippers and the teeny-weeny fairy wing had all disappeared.

"Look Hattie! They've gone! The little people must have taken them. Is that proof?"

"Yes Edward!" gasped Hattie, "I think it is!"

The End

THE BIG HILL

PLAYGROUND